Sleepytime Stories

Margaret Mayo
Illustrated by Penny Dann

PROSPERO
B·O·O·K·S
A DIVISION OF CHAPTERS INC.

This edition produced in 2000 for Prospero, a division of Chapters Inc.
First published in 1999 in Great Britain by Orchard Books, 96 Leonard Street,
London EC2A 4XD
Text © Margaret Mayo 1999
Illustrations © Penny Dann 1999
The right of Margaret Mayo to be identified as the Author and Penny Dann as
the Illustrator of this Work has been asserted by them in accordance with the
Copyright, Designs and Patents Act, 1988.
ISBN 1 55267 082 1
A CIP catalogue record of this book is available from the British Library.
Printed in Hong Kong/China.

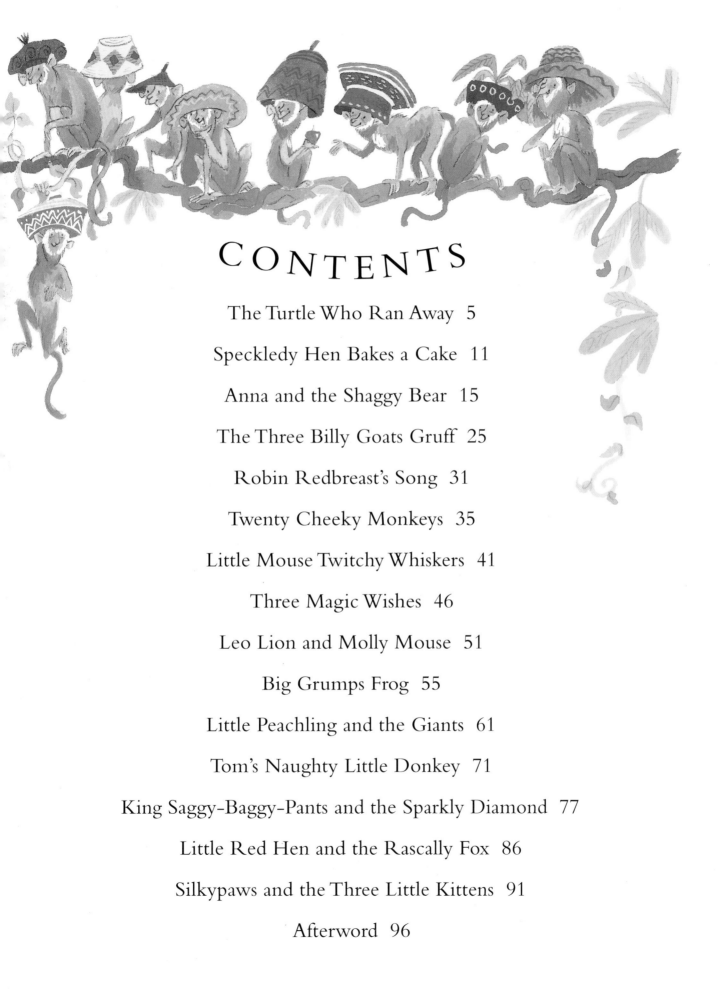

CONTENTS

For Anna and Jack
M.M.

For Isobel and Morgan, with love
P.D.

The Turtle Who Ran Away

LITTLE TURTLE LIVED in a deep, cool river with his mother and father, and most of the time he was a very good little turtle.

Every day he went swimming in the river with his mother and father. They had races. They dived and turned somersaults. They had lots of fun.

Afterwards they climbed on to the river bank and rested under some shady trees. And that's when the big trouble began…because whenever Little Turtle's legs touched dry land, he wanted to run away and *whoof!* he crawled off.

But his mother and father kept their eyes on him, and they quickly chased after and caught him.

His mother always said, "If you run away, Little Turtle, the hot sun will roast you and toast you."

"And," his father said, "Mr Coyote will catch you."

"This river is your home," they both said.

"East, west! Home is best!"

One hot sunny day Little Turtle was crawling by the river bank, and he felt very running-awayish. He looked. He couldn't see his mother. Good. He looked. He couldn't see his father. Even better. And *whoof!* he was off.

He crawled under the shady trees by the river and through a field of grass, until he came to a sandy, stony hill. Then he crawled up the hill.

But after a while Little Turtle began to feel the hot sun beat down on his shell, and the sand beneath his tummy felt hot too.

"I must go home," he said, "before I get roasted and toasted." And he turned round, and began to crawl back.

When he came to a big rock, he stopped to rest. But poor Little Turtle felt so roasted, so toasted and so tired that he began to cry, "*Boo-hooooo…*"

Now on the other side of that rock, fast asleep, was…MR COYOTE. And Little Turtle's crying woke him. Mr Coyote was very cross.

"Be quiet!" he shouted.

But Little Turtle went on: "*Boo-hooo-hoooo…*"

"Stop singing that awful song!" shouted Mr Coyote.

"I'm not singing," said Little Turtle. "I'm crying. *Boo-hoooo…*"

When Mr Coyote heard Little Turtle speak, he licked his lips with his long, thin, pink tongue, and crept round to the other side of the rock.

"You're the one that woke me!" he said. "Well, well…you have made me so cross…so cross…that I AM GOING TO EAT YOU UP!"

Now Little Turtle was very little, BUT he was very clever.

"Eat me if you like!" he said. "But tough luck, Mr Coyote! I've got a hard shell on my back that will crack your teeth and smash them to pieces."

"I won't eat you then," said Mr Coyote. "I shall… THROW YOU IN THE SUN SO YOU'LL BE ABSOLUTELY ROASTED AND TOASTED!"

"Throw me in the sun if you like!" said Little Turtle. "But tough luck, Mr Coyote! I've got this hard shell and I can pop my head under it and hide. You can do anything you like only…only…"

"ONLY WHAT?" said Mr Coyote.

"Only, please don't throw me in the river," said Little Turtle. "Especially not in the deep place under the shady trees."

"Uh-huh…not in the deep place under the shady trees. That's exactly what I'll do," said Mr Coyote. "I'LL THROW YOU IN THE RIVER AT THAT DEEP PLACE AND DROWN YOU!"

Mr Coyote picked up Little Turtle very gently, because Mr Coyote didn't want to smash his teeth. He ran down the sandy, stony hill and through the field of grass. He came to the river, and right at the deepest part, under the shady trees, he threw Little Turtle in…S-P-L-A-S-H!

Little Turtle dived down into the lovely cool water, and he felt fresh and good and all better again. Then he swam up and poked his head above the water.

"Tough luck, Mr Coyote!" he called out. "Tough luck! This river is where I live. Thank you for taking me home!"

Mr Coyote was cross, cross, CROSS! He snapped and snarled. But he couldn't touch Little Turtle. That Little Turtle was safe, safe, SAFE!

Then Little Turtle dived down again, turned three somersaults, swam off and found his mother and father.

"We've been looking everywhere for you," said his mother. "We thought you'd run away and the hot sun had roasted and toasted you!"

"Or Mr Coyote had caught you!" said his father.

"Me? Run away? I don't think I'll run away…not ever again!" said Little Turtle. "East, west! Home is best!"

Speckledy Hen
Bakes a Cake

SPECKLEDY HEN and her five fluffy chicks lived in a little house with Spotted Dog, Ginger Cat and Pink Pig. Speckledy Hen always did all the work, while Spotted Dog, Ginger Cat and Pink Pig did none.

One day Speckledy Hen decided to bake a cake, and she said, "Now who will help me mix the cake?"

"I won't," said Spotted Dog. "I want to play with my bone."

"I won't," said Ginger Cat. "I want to play with my ball."

"And I won't," said Pink Pig. "I want to roll in the grass."

"Then I'll do it myself!" said Speckledy Hen.

So she mixed the butter, sugar, eggs and flour, and her five fluffy chicks gathered round and they tried to help. *Cheep! cheep! cheep!*

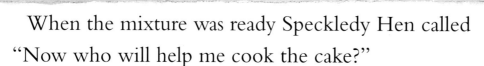

When the mixture was ready Speckledy Hen called "Now who will help me cook the cake?"

"I won't," said Spotted Dog. "I want to go for a run."

I won't

I won't

"I won't," said Ginger Cat. "I want to climb a tree."

And I won't

"And I won't," said Pink Pig. "I want to go for a walk."

"Then I'll do it myself!" said Speckledy Hen.

And she poured the mixture into a tin, popped the tin in the hot oven, and her five fluffy chicks gathered round, and they tried to help. *Cheep! cheep! cheep!*

When the cake was golden-brown and ready, Speckledy Hen took it out of the oven and she called, "Now who will help me set the table?"

"I won't," said Spotted Dog. "I'm tired, and I want to sleep."

"I won't," said Ginger Cat. "I'm tired, and I want to sleep."

"And I won't," said Pink Pig. "I'm tired too, and I want to sleep."

"Then I'll do it myself!" said Speckledy Hen.
And she did, and her five fluffy chicks tried to
help. *Cheep! cheep! cheep!*

"Now," said Speckledy Hen, "who will help me
EAT the cake?"

"I will!" cried Spotted
Dog, jumping up and
wagging his tail.

"I will!" cried Ginger
Cat, jumping up and
licking her lips.

"And I will!" cried
Pink Pig, jumping up
and grunting.

"Oh no, you won't!" said Speckledy
Hen. And she called her five fluffy chicks.

Then Speckledy Hen and her five fluffy chicks ate all
the cake…every tiny crumb!

Anna and the and the Shaggy Bear

ONCE UPON A TIME there was a little girl called
Anna who lived with her grandma and grandpa and
a big bouncy dog in a cottage beside a forest.

One morning Anna's friends knocked at the door
and asked her to come and pick wild strawberries in
the forest. But her grandma said, "No, you can't go.
You're only little. You might get lost."

Anna wanted to go so much that she kept asking, on
and on, until Grandma said, "All right. But you must
keep close to the paths and stay with your friends."

Quickly – before Grandma changed her mind – Anna
tied a red flowery headscarf under her chin, picked up
Grandma's basket, and skipped off with her friends.

At first Anna was careful. She kept close to the paths
and stayed with her friends. But, after a while, she saw
some strawberries in among the trees, and she skipped
over and picked them. She saw some more further on,
and she skipped over and picked them too.

When her basket was almost full, she looked around. But she couldn't see her friends. She listened. But she couldn't hear them. She called, "WHERE – ARE – YOU?" But they didn't answer. So she walked back the way she thought she had come. But there were trees everywhere, and she didn't find the path. And though she called and called, she didn't find her friends.

After a while evening came, and it grew dark, so Anna decided to climb a tree. "In the morning," she said, "my grandma and grandpa and our big bouncy dog will come looking, and they will find me."

She put her basket of strawberries on the ground and climbed a tall tree and sat down on a strong branch. She tried to be brave, but she was cold and hungry, and she began to cry.

Presently a shaggy bear came trotting by. He heard Anna crying and looked up. "Little girl," he said, "what's the matter?"

"I'm lost," said Anna. "I don't know the way home."

"Come down, little girl," said the bear. "I'll carry you to my house, and tomorrow I'll take you home."

He spoke so kindly that Anna climbed down. The bear bent low, and Anna jumped on his back. He picked up the basket of strawberries and trotted off to his house, deep in the forest.

The next day Anna and the bear had strawberries for breakfast. When they had finished, Anna said, "Now, please, Shaggy Bear, take me home."

"I'm too busy today," said the bear. "So be a good little
girl and light the stove and cook some porridge for
our dinner."

Then the bear trotted off into the forest. And Anna lit
the stove and cooked some porridge.

The next morning Anna said, "Please, Shaggy Bear,
take me home."

But the bear said, "No, I won't! I want you to stay here
always and light the stove and cook my dinner!"

Anna kept asking, on and on. But the bear just
said, "NO – I – WON'T!"

Every morning she asked him to take her
home, and he still said, "NO – I – WON'T!"

One morning Anna said, "If you won't take me back to my grandma and grandpa, I shall bake some cherry pies and put them in a basket. Then you must take them to their cottage and leave them on the doorstep, so they'll know I am alive and well.

"All right," said the bear. "I'll do that."

"You must keep your promise, Shaggy Bear," said Anna, "because I'll be watching you. I shall climb to the tip-top of the cherry tree in your garden and keep my eyes on you every step of the way."

As soon as the bear trotted off into the forest, Anna picked some cherries and made some pies. When they were all baked and ready, she wrapped them in her red flowery headscarf. And then – guess what she did – she climbed into Grandma's basket, curled up small and covered herself with the red flowery headscarf that was full of cherry pies.

When the bear came back and saw the basket, he prowled around. *Sniff! sniff! sniff!* "Something smells good," he said, and bent down to look inside.

But a loud voice said: "Shaggy Bear! Don't touch! Those pies are for my grandma and grandpa and nobody else in the world. Pick up the basket, Shaggy Bear, and off you go!"

"My! Oh my!" he growled. "That little girl has got eyes everywhere. Best do what she says." So he picked up the basket and trotted off, towards Anna's cottage.

When he was halfway there, he sat down. "Time to taste one of those cherry pies," he said.

But a loud voice said: "Shaggy Bear! Don't touch! Those pies are for my grandma and grandpa and nobody else in the world. Up you get, Shaggy Bear, and off you go!"

"My! Oh my!" he growled. "That little girl has got eyes everywhere."

He picked up the basket and trotted off, until he came to the door of Anna's cottage. Then he put the basket down. "Now I'll taste one of those pies," he said.

But a loud voice said: "Shaggy Bear! Don't touch! Those pies are for my grandma and grandpa and nobody else in the world. Off you go, Shaggy Bear! Back to your own house!"

"Don't care who they're for!" growled the bear. "I'm hungry!"

He reached out a paw…he touched the red flowery headscarf. But next moment…a big bouncy dog bounded round the corner of the the cottage *slap-bang!* into the bear and almost knocked him over. "*Wuff! wuff!*" barked the dog. "*Wuff! wuff! wuff!*"

The bear didn't know who this big bouncy creature was that had slap-banged into him. And he didn't stop to find out. He trotted off, back to the forest growling, "My! Oh my! That little girl has got eyes everywhere! My! Oh my!"

And Anna never saw that shaggy bear ever again!

Well, next thing…the cottage door opened…and there
stood Anna's grandma and grandpa. Then Anna climbed
out of the basket, and in her hands she held the red
flowery headscarf, full of cherry pies.

"I've brought you a present," she said.

And you can guess what happened next. Lots of hugs!
Lots of kisses! And the big bouncy dog joined in! He
gave Anna licky kisses all over.

Then they went into the cottage and ate cherry pies.
Grandpa ate three, Grandma ate two, and Anna was so
happy and excited that she could only manage one.
But the big bouncy dog made up for her. He ate six,
because those cherry pies that Anna made tasted really,
truly delicious.

The Three Billy Goats Gruff

ONCE UPON A TIME there were three billy goats who had curly horns on top of their heads and tufty beards under their chins. They were brothers, and the name of all three was Gruff.

There was Little Billy Goat Gruff, Middle Size Billy Goat Gruff and Great Big Billy Goat Gruff. And they all lived beside a hill where the grass was juicy and green.

One fine day, the three billy goats decided to climb the hill and eat lots of juicy grass and grow fat.

But on the way they had to cross a rickety-rackety bridge over a stream, and under that bridge lived… an ugly, wicked Troll, who had eyes as big as saucers, a nose as long as a poker and teeth as sharp as knives.

Well, Little Billy Goat Gruff started off first – trot, trot over the rickety-rackety bridge – and the bridge went *trip-trap! trip-trap!*

Then the Troll under the bridge roared, "Who's that trip-trapping on my bridge?"

"It's only Little Billy Goat Gruff. I'm going to climb the hill and eat grass and grow fat," said Little Billy Goat Gruff in a tiny voice.

"Ho! ho!" roared the Troll. "I'm coming to gobble you up!"

"Oh, don't do that. I'm too little to eat," said Little Billy Goat Gruff. "Wait till my brother Middle Size Billy Goat Gruff comes. He's much bigger than me."

"BIGGER than you, is he?" said the Troll. "All right then. Off you go!"

Not long after, along came Middle Size Billy Goat Gruff
– TROT, TROT over the rickety-rackety bridge – and the
bridge went *TRIP-TRAP! TRIP-TRAP!*

The Troll under the bridge roared, "Who's that TRIP-
TRAPPING on my bridge!"

"It's only Middle Size Billy Goat Gruff. I'm going to
climb the hill and eat grass and grow fat," said Middle Size
Billy Goat Gruff, in a middle-size sort of voice.

"Ho! ho!" roared the Troll. "I'm coming
to gobble you up!"

"Oh, don't do that. I'm too little
to eat," said Middle Size Billy
Goat Gruff. "Wait till my
brother Great Big Billy Goat
Gruff comes. He's much
bigger than me."

"BIGGER than you, is
he?" said the Troll.
"All right then.
Off you go!"

Not long after, along came Great Big Billy Goat Gruff –
TRAMP, STAMP over the rickety-rackety bridge – and
the bridge went *TRAMP-STAMP! TRAMP-STAMP!*

The Troll under the bridge roared, "Who's that
TRAMP-STAMPING on my bridge?"

"IT IS I! GREAT BIG BILLY GOAT GRUFF!" said
Great Big Billy Goat Gruff in a great big gruff voice.

"Ho! ho!" roared the Troll. "I'm coming to gobble
you up!"

"COME ON THEN!" said Great Big Billy Goat Gruff.
The ugly, wicked Troll climbed up on to the bridge. But
Great Big Billy Goat Gruff…he just lowered his head with
the curly horns on top…and one! two! three! he charged
and tossed that Troll over the bridge and
SPLOSH! into the
stream below.

Then Great Big Billy Goat Gruff climbed the hill
and joined his brothers.

And those three billy goats lived on that hill, happy
as could be, eating lots of juicy grass – and they all
grew nice and fat!

Robin Redbreast's Song

ONE BRIGHT, SUNNY DAY Robin Redbreast was so happy he hopped on a rose bush, and he sang a good song.

Just then, along strolled Thomas Cat, and he said, very friendly like, "Now tell me, Robin Redbreast, what are you doing up in that thorny rose bush?"

"I'm singing a happy song, this bright, sunny day," chirped Robin Redbreast.

"Come here…" said Thomas Cat. "Come…and I'll show you the beautiful white fur that grows under my chin."

"No, no, sly Thomas Cat Sharp-claws," said Robin Redbreast. "No! No! You may catch a little mouse that way but you won't catch me!"

And he bobbed his tail, and *whoo-oops!* away he flew.

When he came to a river, he landed on a bramble bush growing beside the water, and again he sang his good song.

Just then down flew Howard Hawk, and he said, very friendly like, "Now tell me, Robin Redbreast, what are you doing in among those prickly brambles?"

"I'm singing a happy song, this bright, sunny day," chirped Robin Redbreast.

"Come here..." said Howard Hawk. "Come...and I'll show you the beautiful grey feather that grows under my wing."

"No, no, sly Howard Hawk Sharp-beak," said Robin Redbreast. "No! No! You may catch a little sparrow that way but you won't catch me!"

And he bobbed his tail, and *whoo-oops!* away he flew.

When he came to a hill, he landed on a high rock, and again he sang his good song.

Just then along strolled Frederick Fox, and he said, very friendly like, "Now tell me, Robin Redbreast, what are you doing up on that high rock?"

"I'm singing a happy song, this bright, sunny day," chirped Robin Redbreast.

"Come here…" said Frederick Fox. "Come…and I'll show you the beautiful white fur that grows at the tip of my tail."

"No, no, sly Frederick Fox Sharp-teeth," said Robin Redbreast. "No! No! You may catch a little lamb that way but you won't catch me!"

And he bobbed his tail, and *whoo-oops!* away he flew.

When he came to a house, he landed on the windowsill, and again he sang his good song.

33

Just then, inside the house, a little boy and a little girl looked up from playing with their toys.

The little boy smiled. "There's Robin Redbreast," he said, "sitting on our windowsill."

"And he's singing a song for us!" laughed the little girl. "Now what can we give to Robin Redbreast."

And do you know what those two little children did? They filled a bag with breadcrumbs, and crept into the garden and scattered the crumbs on the grass. Then they kept as quiet and still as they could.

Robin Redbreast flew down, and he ate and he ate. When he was full, he bobbed his tail, and *whoo-oops!* he flew up into a rowan tree.

And then he sang for the little children his best and sweetest and longest song, that bright, sunny day!

Twenty Cheeky Monkeys

ONCE THERE WAS a small girl who loved wearing hats. Red, green and yellow. Blue and purple. Stripy hats. Zig-zaggy patterned hats. Embroidered hats. Any kind of hat. She just loved putting a hat on her head. It made her feel grand and grown-up.

The girl, whose name was Ngozi, was lucky, because her mother made hats. So there were always lots of beautiful hats at home to try on.

Every few weeks, Ngozi's mother piled the
hats she had made into a basket, and swung it up
on top of her head. Ngozi tied her baby brother on
to her back. And then off they walked, along the
path, through the jungly forest,
till they came to the market
where they sold the hats.

Ngozi loved that too.
The market was such a
busy, noisy place to be.

But one time, when market
day came round, baby brother was
sick, and Ngozi's mother decided to stay at home and look
after him.

"I want you to take the hats to market and sell them,"
she said. "Can you do that?"

"Oh, yes!" said Ngozi.

"There are twenty-one hats. Now don't lose any!"

"Oh, no!" said Ngozi.

Then her mother piled the twenty-one hats into
the basket. Ngozi swung it up on her head, and off she
walked along the path through the jungly forest.

But baby brother had kept her awake most of the night with his crying, and she soon felt tired and wanted to rest. So when she came to a clearing in the jungly forest, she put her basket on the ground and sat down. She reached over and chose her favourite hat. It was a red, yellow and green one, with a black and white zig-zaggy pattern. She put the hat on her head, rested her back against a tree, closed her eyes and fell asleep.

After a while she woke. She rubbed her sleepy eyes, stretched and stood up. She reached over to the basket…but…there were no hats inside. It was empty.

She looked on the grass. No hats. She looked up – and what did she see? A whole troop of monkeys sitting in the trees…and every monkey had a HAT on its head. Just like Ngozi.

Then she knew what had happened. Those cheeky monkeys had crept down while she was sleeping. Every one had chosen a hat, put it on and climbed back up again.

Ngozi was so upset, she shook a fist at them and shouted: "Give me back my hats!"

But all the monkeys just shook a fist and shouted back: "*Jibba! jibba! jibba!*"

Ngozi stamped her feet and shouted: "Give me back my hats!"

And all the monkeys jumped up and down on the branches and shouted: "*Jibba! jibba! jibba!*"

Ngozi patted her hat and shouted: "Give me back my hats!"

Then the monkeys patted their hats and shouted: "*Jibba! jibba! jibba!*"

Now what could she do? She had lost twenty hats. What would her mother say? Ngozi was so very upset she snatched her hat off her head and flung it on the ground.

Then…twenty monkeys snatched their hats off their heads. Just like Ngozi. And twenty hats…came flying through the air and landed on the ground.

Quick! quick! Ngozi picked up the hats and piled them into the basket. "Goodbye, you cheeky monkeys!" she called, and gave them a wave.

The twenty cheeky monkeys shouted: "*Jibba! jibba! jibba!*" And they waved. Just like Ngozi.

Quick! quick! she hurried off to the market. And, do you know, she sold every hat in the basket. Twenty-one hats!

She was so happy, she smiled all the way home. And when she got there, baby brother was well again — and he was smiling.

Ngozi's mother was smiling too! "You sold every hat!" she said. "You didn't lose any! I am so pleased, I'm going to make an extra-special hat. Just for you. Choose your favourite colours."

Ngozi chose red, yellow and green. "And can you put a black and white zig-zaggy pattern on it?" she asked.

"Of course I can," said her mother.

When the extra-special hat was ready, Ngozi put it on her head. Then she walked about, nose in the air, and she felt extra-specially grand and grown-up.

Little Mouse Twitchy Whiskers

ONE DAY A little mouse called Twitchy Whiskers was running through the woods when she saw an old cardboard box. She stopped and twitched her whiskers and said: "What's this – a warm house? It looks just right for one mouse!"

Then she snuffled all around the box and twitched her whiskers again and called out: "Who lives in this house?"

But no one answered.

So she crept inside.

After a while a frog came by, and when he saw the box he called out: "Who lives in this house?"

"Twitchy Whiskers lives here," said the little mouse. "And who are you?"

"I am the Croaking Frog," he said. "Please let me in."

"Come in," said Twitchy Whiskers. "Now we are two."

And the frog hopped inside.

After a while a rabbit came by, and when he saw the box he called out: "Who lives in this house?"

"Twitchy Whiskers and the Croaking Frog live here," said the little mouse. "And who are you?"

"I'm the Jumping Rabbit," he said. "Please let me in."

"Come in," said Twitchy Whiskers. "Now we are three."

And the rabbit jumped inside.

After a while a hen came by, and when she saw the box she called out: "Who lives in this house?"

"Twitchy Whiskers and the Croaking Frog and the Jumping Rabbit live here," said the little mouse. "And who are you?"

"I'm the Clucking Hen," she said. "Please let me in."

"Come in," said Twitchy Whiskers. "Now we are four."

And the hen bustled inside.

After a while a duck came by, and when she saw the box, she called out: "Who lives in this house?"

"Twitchy Whiskers and the Croaking Frog and the Jumping Rabbit and the Clucking Hen live here," said the little mouse. "And who are you?"

"I am the Waddling Duck," she said. "Please let me in."

"Come in," said Twitchy Whiskers. "Now we are five."

And the duck waddled inside.

There wasn't much room. But they curled up small and squeezed up tight and somehow everyone fitted in.

Then a bear came by, and when he saw the box he called out: "Who lives in this house?"

"Twitchy Whiskers and the Croaking Frog and the Jumping Rabbit and the Clucking Hen and the Waddling Duck live here," said the little mouse. "And who are you?"

The bear said, "I am Bear Big-and-Fat who can squash you all flat, so LET ME IN!"

"I am sorry," said Twitchy Whiskers, "but the house is full. We are curled up small and squeezed up tight and the house is stretched to bursting. So we cannot let you in."

The bear growled, loud as he could: "Rumbling thunder! I'll tumble you under! This Bear Big-and-Fat will SQUASH YOU ALL FLAT!"

Then Twitchy Whiskers and the frog and the rabbit and the hen and the duck opened their eyes very wide, and they saw that bear coming down…down…down…right on top of their house. So out they tumbled and off they ran, this way and that way.

And the bear sat down on the house *whumpf!* – and he squashed it all flat.

But he did *not* squash Twitchy Whiskers and the Croaking Frog and the Jumping Rabbit and the Clucking Hen and the Waddling Duck. He did *not* squash them flat.

They all got back to their own homes, safe and sound.

Three Magic Wishes

JACK WAS a poor woodcutter who lived with his wife, Mary, in a little log hut beside a forest.

One day, when he was deep in the forest cutting down trees, he saw a big old tree he hadn't noticed before.

"That's a fine tree," he said. "I'll cut it down."

He swung his axe over his shoulder and was just going to wham it down when a small soft voice called, "Stop, Mr Woodcutter! Don't cut down this tree!"

Then Jack saw, way up in the branches, a teeny, tiny man. He was dressed in green, except for his pointy brown slippers, while in his hands he held a pointy red hat. The teeny, tiny man was a woodland elf.

"I wouldn't chop down your house, Mr Woodcutter," said the elf. "So, please, don't chop down mine. This big tree is where I live."

Jack frowned and scratched his head. "*Whoo!* If you live here," he said, "of course I won't chop the tree down!"

"Then you shall have a thank-you present," said the elf. "You shall have three magic wishes. But, Mr Woodcutter, be careful how you use them!"

With that the elf stuck the pointy red hat firmly on his head and was gone. Maybe you have guessed – it was a magic hat, and when the elf put it on nobody could see him.

When Jack got home to his little hut that evening, he was very hungry, and the first thing he said was: "What's for supper, Mary?"

"Cabbage soup," she said.

"Not cabbage soup again!" grumbled Jack. "I wish I had a big fat sausage!"

And *pfff!* a frying pan, with a sausage in it going *sizzle-sizzle!* came flying through the air, and landed on the stove.

"Oh! That's one wish gone!" said Jack. "I quite forgot." And then he told Mary about the elf and the three magic wishes.

"Three magic wishes, and you wasted one on a SAUSAGE!" cried Mary. "You could have wished for a new house, or some money. I am so cross, I wish… I-wish-that-sausage-was-stuck-on-your-nose!"

And *pfff!* the sausage jumped up and stuck itself on the end of Jack's nose.

"Oh! That's two wishes gone!" said Jack. "Now what shall we do? I can't go round with a big fat sausage stuck on my nose!"

"I'll pull it off," said Mary. And she grabbed the sausage and pulled. But it was stuck fast on his nose. She couldn't move it.

"I'll cut it off," said Mary.

"No! You might cut off my nose," cried Jack. "There is only one thing we can do. I'll have to use the last wish."

"Oh, no!" cried Mary.

"Oh, yes!" said Jack. "I-wish-the-sausage-was-off-my-nose-and-in-the-frying-pan!"

And *pfff!* the sausage jumped off his nose, and there it was in the frying-pan, going *sizzle-sizzle!*

"So – that's the three wishes gone," said Jack. "But we do have a big fat sausage for supper and not CABBAGE SOUP!"

Then Jack and Mary sat down and shared the sausage. And it was the juiciest, yummiest sausage they had ever tasted. Of course, it had to be! It was a magic sausage! And they are the best.

So now, when you meet a woodland elf, and *pfff!* he gives you three magic wishes, think carefully before you decide what you would like to have.

Leo Lion and Molly Mouse

Iт was a hot, sunshiny day in the forest, and Leo, the big strong lion was tired. "Time for my afternoon nap," he said. And he stretched out, closed his eyes and fell asleep.

In the same forest lived Molly, a little frisky–whisky mouse, and she wasn't a bit sleepy.

She frisked and whisked among the trees, playing games. She was having such fun, until she frisked and whisked on to something soft and warm. What was it? Oh! oh! she was standing on one of Leo Lion's big paws.

She was so frightened that she squealed, "*Ee-eek! Ee-eek!*"

Leo Lion opened his eyes, lifted his other paw, and he grabbed Molly Mouse and held her tight.

"*ARR-RRR!*" he roared. "You woke me!" He was very angry, and he scooped her up and nearly popped her into his big mouth.

"*Ee-eeek!*" she squealed. "Please don't eat me. I want to be your friend."

"You? My friend? Ho! ho! ho!" he laughed. "You're too little to be my friend."

"If you're kind and let me go," she said, "I'll pay you back one day. I'll be your friend. I will."

"Ho! ho! ho!" laughed Leo Lion. "You're such a funny little mouse that I'm going to let you go anyway." And he gently dropped her on the ground.

"Thank you," said Molly Mouse. "I'll pay you back. I will. I won't forget."

And off she scampered.

A few days later, Molly Mouse was frisking and whisking as usual, when she heard a loud roar: "*ARR-RRR! HOO-ARRR!*"

"That's Leo Lion," she said. "I wonder what's the matter? He sounds upset."

And off she scampered, until she found him.

Big strong Leo Lion was all caught up inside a net made of thick ropes. It held him tight.

He gave a roary groan, "*HOO-OO-ARRR…* I stepped into a trap… a hunter's trap…and I can't get out…"

"I'll help you," said Molly Mouse. "I'll get you out."

"But how?" groaned Leo Lion. "You're so very little."

"Watch me," said Molly Mouse.

She frisked and whisked over to the net, and with her small sharp teeth began to gnaw, gnaw, gnaw…and at last she gnawed right through one thick rope. Gnaw, gnaw, gnaw…and she gnawed through another thick rope…and then another and another until at last…Leo Lion was free.

"Thank you!" he said. "You are a very kind, clever little mouse."

"You were kind. You didn't eat me. And I promised to pay you back," said Molly Mouse. "Now – are we friends?"

"Yes," said Leo Lion. "We are friends."

And, from then on, Leo Lion and Molly Mouse were the best of friends.

Big Grumps Frog

ONE MORNING FROG woke up, and very first thing
he had the big grumps. It was Kookaburra's fault. As usual
he was sitting up in a gum tree laughing his loud chuckly
laugh: "*Gah! gah! gah!*"

"You woke me up," grumped Frog. "Stop that laughing
noise…I want to sleep…"

But Kookaburra went on laughing: "*Gah! gah! gah!*"

"Stop that laughing noise now," grumped Frog, "or
you'll be sorry. You will."

But Kookaburra just went on laughing: "*Gah! gah! gah!*"

Frog had had enough. "Right then…I warned you…"
he grumped. "So look out…here comes trouble…"

And what did Frog do? He hopped down to his favourite pool, and *shhh-lurp!* he drank and drank. And – goodness gracious! he stretched, stretched, stretched until he was VERY LARGE.

Kookaburra stopped laughing. "Don't do that!" he called out. "Don't drink all the water!"

But Frog drank the pool dry. He hopped slowly over to a stream, and *shhh-lurp!* he drank and drank. And – goodness gracious! he stretched, stretched, stretched until he was ABSOLUTELY ENORMOUS.

All the birds and animals came flying, running, wriggling, jumping. "Don't do that!" they called out. "Don't drink all the water!"

But Frog drank the stream dry. He hopped slowly off, and *shhh-lurp! shhh-lurp! shhh-lurp!* he drank up every pool and every stream. And – goodness gracious! he stretched, stretched, stretched until he was ABSOLUTELY GIGANTIC.

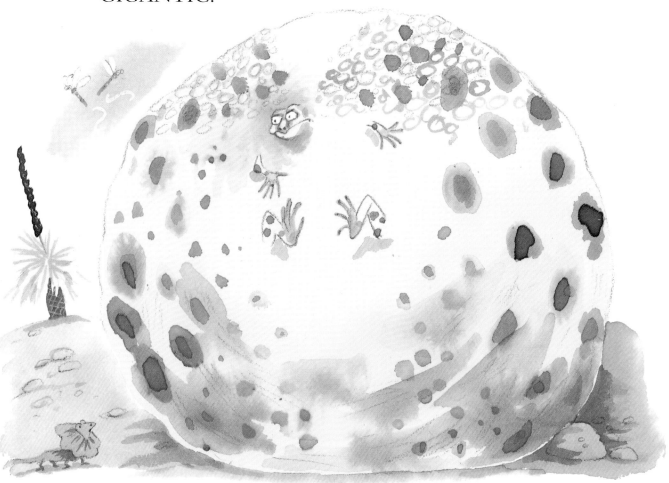

Now there was no water anywhere for the birds and animals to drink, and they were thirsty.

"Frog," they called. "Please, Frog, give us back the water."

But Frog still had the big grumps. And he just kept his mouth tight shut and blinked his eyes.

"We must do something to get the water out of him," said Strong-tailed Kangaroo. "Maybe I should jump on him."

"I could bite him," said Wild-dog Dingo.

"I could prick him," said Spiny Ant-eater.

"Or we could make him laugh," said Kookaburra.

"Then he would have to open his mouth, and the water would come shooting out."

"Yes! yes!" the others agreed. "Let's have a Great Laugh-about!"

So then a Great Laugh-about began. Everyone took turns and did something funny. Long-legged Emu did a wibbly-wobbly walk. Wild-dog Dingo told jokes. Strong-tailed Kangaroo did a jumping dance. Shiny-nose Koala played peek-a-boo in a gum tree. Spiny Ant-eater rattled his spines. Duck-billed Platypus told a funny story. And Kookaburra sang his laughing song.

Everyone laughed a lot – except for Frog. He still had the big grumps. And he just kept his mouth tight shut and blinked his eyes.

At last everyone had had a turn, except Black Eel. She was shy. "I'm not very good at doing funny things," she whispered. "But I could try to do my wriggle dance."

"You can't dance!" said Kookaburra. "You haven't any legs!"

"Well, I could wriggle and wiggle, and then I could…" She whispered something to Kookaburra.

"Sure! You could try that!" said Kookaburra.

Black Eel wriggled and wiggled, over to Frog. And when she was right up close…guess what she did…wriggly, wiggly, very fast…she tickled his tummy! Then…wriggly, wiggly, faster and faster…she tickled him all over his gigantic tummy!

Frog grinned. He began to giggle. He couldn't help it. His mouth burst open and he laughed out loud. And then – all the water came shooting out, and *splishity-splosh!* away it tumbled and filled up every stream and every pool.

"Stop tickling me…please…stop..." laughed Frog.

"Have the big grumps gone?" whispered shy Black Eel.

"Big grumps…all gone," he laughed.

"Good!" whispered shy Black Eel. And she stopped her tickling.

"Well done, Black Eel!" said Kookaburra. "Well done! And now it's time for us all to have a drink!"

Then all the birds and animals went flying, running, wriggling, jumping off to their own favourite stream or pool, and they had a long, long drink.

Even Frog hopped over to his favourite pool and had a drink. But this time he only had one very small *shhh-lurp!*

Little Peachling and the Giants

ONCE UPON A TIME there lived a poor old man and a poor old woman who were very sad because they had no children.

One day the old woman decided to do some washing, so she piled the dirty clothes into a basket, and off she went down to the river. There she slish-sloshed and rub-rub-rubbed until the clothes were clean.

She had just piled everything back in the basket, when she saw something floating down the river. It was a big, rosy red peach. It floated closer. The old woman reached out, and it floated…*right into her hands!*

"This is my good-luck day!" she said. And she tucked the peach in among the clothes, picked up the basket and hurried home.

As soon as she saw the old man, she called out: "Look what I found in the river!"

"What a big, rosy red peach!" said the old man. "Let's cut it up and eat it!"

But the next moment…the peach burst open…and inside it was…*a little baby boy!*

"Ohhh! At last we have a baby of our own!" exclaimed the old woman. "What shall we call him?"

"We'll call him Little Peachling," said the old man. "Because we found him in a peach, and he is very little."

And that was the name they gave him.

Well, Little Peachling was a hungry baby. He ate one half of the peach, he ate the other half, and he grew. He ate a bowl of rice and a bowl of fish, and he grew and grew. Never has a baby eaten so much or grown so fast.

Soon he could walk and talk, and before long he was a tall strong boy. The old man and the old woman loved him very much. And he loved them back, and always called them Grandfather and Grandmother, because they were old.

Now not far off, in a castle by the sea, lived some wicked giants. They were forever stomping out of their castle and stealing money, jewels, any treasures they could find. Everyone was afraid of them.

One day Little Peachling bowed his head and said most politely, "Grandfather, Grandmother, I must go to the giants' castle and stop their wickedness."

The old man shook his head slowly and said:

"The giants are tough, and they're wicked too!
You'd better take care or they might
kill you!"

But Little Peachling said "I'm not scared of them!"

"Little Peachling!" cried the old woman, "Bravest Boy! Number One Hero!"

Then she gave him new trousers and tied a scarf about his head. She cooked some rice cakes and put them in a bag and hung it from his belt. And then he was ready.

"Goodbye! goodbye!" he called as he jogged off.

"Good luck!" they called after him.

Little Peachling hadn't gone far when a big yellow dog came running from among the tall grass.

"*Woo-oof!* I am Fiercest Dog," he barked. "Where are you going?"

"To the giants' castle!" said Little Peachling.

Fiercest Dog said:

"The giants are tough and they're wicked too!
But give me a rice cake, and I'll come with you!"

So Little Peachling gave him a rice cake, and they jogged off.

They hadn't gone far when a
red-capped pheasant flew down.

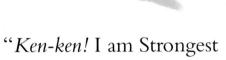

"*Ken-ken!* I am Strongest
Pheasant," he screeched. "Where are you going?"

"To the giants' castle," said Little Peachling.

Strongest Pheasant said:

"*The giants are tough and they're wicked too!*

But give me a rice cake, and I'll come with you!"

So Little Peachling gave him a rice cake, Strongest
Pheasant perched on his shoulder, and they all jogged off.

They hadn't gone far when a grey monkey swung
down from a tree.

"*Kia-kia!* I am Cleverest
Monkey," he chattered.
"Where are you going?"

"To the giants' castle," said
Little Peachling.

Cleverest Monkey said:

"*The giants are tough and they're wicked too!*

But give me a rice cake, and I'll come
with you!"

So Little Peachling gave him a rice cake, Cleverest Monkey jumped on Fiercest Dog's back, and they all jogged off.

At last they came to a huge castle by the sea. There was a wall around it and a gate, all bolted and barred. So – how could they get in?

Well, Strongest Pheasant flew over the wall. Cleverest Monkey climbed over the gate, pulled back the bolts and bars and opened it. Then Fiercest Dog and Little Peachling jogged in.

But next thing…lots of giants came stomping out of the castle. They were HUGE, and they looked TOUGH and FIERCE.

But Little Peachling sang out:

"You may be tough and wicked too!

But we're Number One Heroes and not scared of you!"

Then the fight began. Fiercest Dog bit the giants' ankles.
Strongest Pheasant pecked their noses. Cleverest Monkey
tugged their hair and pinched them. And Little Peachling
wrestled. He tossed a giant – *wheee!* – to one side.
He tossed another giant – *wheee!* – up in the air.
And *wheee! wheee!* he kept on tossing.

Those giants were scared – they ran helter-skelter back into the castle and hid. Only the king of the giants remained.

"Please, don't hurt us," he said. "We'll give you our treasure! As much as you want!"

"All right," said Little Peachling. "Give us a great cart load of treasure, and promise there'll be no more stealing, no more wickedness."

"I promise," said the king of the giants. "We will stop being wicked. We will!" He called the other giants, and they came creeping out of the castle. They quickly found a cart and piled it high with treasure – gold, silver, jade, all sorts of jewels – so much treasure!

Then the heroes were off. Little Peachling and Fiercest Dog led the way. Cleverest Monkey sat on top of the treasure, while Strongest Pheasant pulled the cart, and the wheels went round *kirro! kirro!*

When Little Peachling came to his own home,
he sang out:

"We've beaten the giants and scared them too!
They never again will steal from you!"

"Little Peachling!" cried the old woman. "Bravest Boy!
Number One Hero!"

But Little Peachling said, "Grandmother, here are three
other Number One Heroes – Fiercest Dog, Strongest
Pheasant and Cleverest Monkey! Without their help,
I could not have beaten the giants!"

Then off went the three helpers.
Their work was done.

"Goodbye Little
Peachling!" they
called. "Goodbye!"

And did those giants keep their promise?
Yes, they did. They stopped doing wicked things.

So from then on, the old man and the old woman lived
in peace. They had plenty of everything. But, best of all,
they had their own son – Little Peachling.

Tom's Naughty Little Donkey

ONCE THERE WAS a boy called Tom who lived on a farm, and he had a little grey donkey whose name was Ned.

Every morning Tom took Ned out of the stable, up the hill, through a gate and into a field, and all day Ned had fun. He trotted about and flicked his tail. He flip-flopped his long ears and sang a happy donkey song, "*Hee-haw!* Every day, I like to play!" But most of the time, he ate – *munch-munch!* – grass, buttercups and daisies, dandelions and thistles.

In the evening, before it was dark, Tom climbed the hill, opened the gate and called, "Ned! Time to go home!"

And the donkey always sang back, "*Hee-haw!* I'm coming!" And trot, trot he followed Tom back to the stable.

But one evening when Tom called, Ned snorted, "*Honh!* Go away! I want to play!" And he galloped off.

Tom chased him round the field, until Tom was so tired he couldn't run another step.

He was cross. He flumped down on the grass and grumbled, "What a naughty donkey!"

Just then Bossy Goose came waddling by. "Why are you so cross?" she asked.

"I'm cross," said Tom, "because my naughty donkey won't go home."

"I'll hiss and I'll snap! And I'll make him go home!" said Bossy Goose. "Easy-peasy!"

Bossy Goose waddled over to Ned. She stretched out her neck. "*Hs-s-sss!* Go home! Go! go! go!" she hissed. And she tried to snap at his legs with her big sharp beak.

But Ned galloped off, snorting, "*Honh!* Go away! I want to play!"

Bossy Goose was cross. She flumped down beside Tom and grumbled, "What a naughty donkey!"

Not long after, Big Dog came bounding along. "Why are you both so cross?" he asked.

"I'm cross," said Bossy Goose, "because Tom is cross. And Tom is cross because his naughty donkey won't go home!"

"I'll bark and I'll bite! And I'll make him go home," said Big Dog. "Easy-peasy!"

Big Dog bounded over to Ned. "*Woooff!* Go home! Go! go! go!" he barked. And he tried to bite Ned's legs with his big sharp teeth.

But Ned galloped off, snorting, "*Honh!* Go away! I want to play!"

Big Dog was cross. He flumped down beside Bossy Goose and grumbled, "What a naughty donkey!"

Presently Fuzzy Bee came flying by "Oh dear! What is the matter?" he asked. "Why are you all so cross?"

"I'm cross," said Big Dog, "because Bossy Goose is cross. She is cross because Tom is cross. And Tom is cross because his naughty donkey won't go home."

"Cheer up! I'll just do some buzzing and he will go home," said Fuzzy Bee. "Easy-peasy!"

"You're only a small, fuzzy-buzzy sort of thing," said Big Dog. "And you really think you can do something I can't do!"

"And something I can't do!" said Bossy Goose.

"And I can't!" said Tom.

Then they all laughed.

Fuzzy Bee didn't say a word. He flew over to Ned. And *buzz-zip!* Fuzzy Bee zoomed into one long ear, and *buzz-zip!* into the other.

Ned shook his head up and down, side to side. He didn't like the buzzing noise in his ears.

"Time to go home!" said Fuzzy Bee. And again *buzz-zip!* he flew into one ear, and back into the other.

Ned shook his head some more. "All right," he said, "all right. I'm coming!" And he trotted off, through the gate and down the hill, with Fuzzy Bee buzzing after him.

Tom, Bossy Goose and Big Dog looked at each other, their eyes big and round. They were so surprised.

But Tom soon jumped to his feet and chased Ned and Fuzzy Bee all the way back to the stable.

"Clever Fuzzy Bee, thank you for making my naughty donkey go home," said Tom. "Thank you very much."

"Oh, it was easy-peasy!" said Fuzzy Bee and *buzz-zip!* off he flew.

"Now, Ned," said Tom, "are you ready to be a good little donkey that goes straight to bed, with no fuss and bother?"

"*Hee-haw!*" said Ned. "I am!"

Then Ned trotted into the stable and lay down in his bed of fresh straw and went straight to sleep. He was a very, very tired little donkey.

King Saggy-Baggy-Pants
and the Sparkly Diamond

IN A POOR, tumbledown cottage there once lived a boy called Sam and his mother, and they had a little cockerel.

One day the little cockerel hadn't had any breakfast, so he marched out of the garden, crossed the road and scritch-scratched on a rubbish heap, looking for some insects or juicy worms to eat. Suddenly he scratched out something bright and sparkly. It was a DIAMOND. Imagine! A diamond on a rubbish heap!

"I shall give this diamond to Sam and his mother," said the little cockerel. "Then they'll be rich!" And he picked it up in his beak.

At that moment the king strolled by. He was a large king, and he wore large, saggy-baggy silk pants, a large, saggy-baggy silk shirt and a long scarf swirled and twirled around his head. Behind the king strolled three servants, almost as large as the king.

Now when the king saw the little cockerel and the sparkly diamond he said, "Grab the cockerel and bring me the diamond!"

So the three servants grabbed the little cockerel, took the diamond and gave it to the king.

The little cockerel shouted, "That's my diamond! I found it! Give it back!"

The king and his servants hurried off. But the little cockerel chased them helter-skelter on his little legs.

When the king reached the palace, he put the diamond in his treasure chest.

But when the little cockerel reached the palace, he jumped on a windowsill and shouted:

"King Saggy-baggy-pants! Cock-a-doodle-do!

Give me back the diamond! It doesn't belong to you!"

"Grab the cockerel," roared the king. "And toss him in the well and drown him!"

The three large servants ran out and grabbed the cockerel, and they tossed him in the well.

The little cockerel wasn't scared. "Stretchy stomach," he said, "swallow water." He opened his beak and all the water in the well swooshity-swooshed into his stomach.

Then the little cockerel flew out of the well, jumped on the windowsill and shouted again:

"King Saggy-baggy-pants! Cock-a-doodle-do!

Give me back the diamond! It doesn't belong to you!"

"Grab the cockerel," roared the king. "And toss him in the fire and roast him!"

The three large servants ran out and grabbed the cockerel, and they tossed him in the fire.

The little cockerel wasn't a bit scared. "Stretchy stomach," he said, "put out fire." He opened his beak, and all the water in his stomach swooshity-swooshed up and over the fire and put it out.

Then the little cockerel shook his feathers dry, and he marched up to the king's sitting room. He jumped on to the king's very own chair and shouted yet again:

80

"King Saggy-baggy-pants!
Cock-a-doodle-do!
Give me back the diamond!
It doesn't belong to you!"

The king was furious. "Grab the cockerel," he roared. "And…and toss him in the beehive so the bees can sting him to death!"

So the three large servants grabbed the cockerel and stuffed him in the beehive.

But the little cockerel wasn't one tiny bit scared. "Bees," he whispered, "hide among my feathers." And *hmm-mmmmm…* humming softly, the bees crept in among his feathers.

Then the little cockerel flew out of the beehive. He marched into the palace, up to the king's sitting room, jumped on to the king's chair and shouted, the loudest ever:

"King Saggy-baggy-pants!
Cock-a-doodle-do!
Give me back the diamond!
It doesn't belong to you!"

Now the king was even more furious. He roared, "What…WHAT…shall I do with that wretched, pesky cockerel?"

"Cut off his head!" said the first servant.

"Tie him up and hang him on the flag pole!" said the second.

"Sit on him!" said the third. "Squash him flat!"

"That's it!" roared the king. "I'll sit on him and SQUASH HIM FLAT!"

So the three large servants grabbed the cockerel and held him on the chair.

The little cockerel wasn't one tiny bit scared. Not him.

As the king's rather large bottom came down…and down, the little cockerel whispered, "Bees, fly out and sting the king."

And *zoo-oom!* bees swarmed from under his feathers, and flew into…the king's rather large, saggy-baggy pants and…uh-huh!…oh-ho!…guess what!…they STUNG

the king all over…his
rather large bottom.

"*Oww-owww…ouch!*" squealed
the king. He jumped up, and
danced around, waving his
arms. "All right, you wretched,
pesky cockerel, take your
dratted diamond and get
out of my palace!"

So the three large servants took the little cockerel to
the king's treasure room and unlocked the treasure chest.
It was full of silver, gold and all kinds of splendid jewels
which the king had stolen and, right on top, lay the
sparkly diamond.

"Stretchy stomach," said the little cockerel, "suck up
the treasure!" He opened his beak, and first the diamond,
and then the rest of the treasure swooshity-swooshed
into his stomach.

"Tell King Saggy-baggy-pants," said the little cockerel, "that I don't want to see him ever again!"

Then off he marched, back to the poor, tumbledown cottage.

Sam and his mother were very pleased to see him. "But where have you been?" asked Sam.

"Stretchy stomach," said the little cockerel, "show him what you've got!"

Then silver, gold, all kinds of splendid jewels, and, finally, the sparkly diamond swooshity-swooshed out of his beak and on to the floor.

"Terrific!" gasped Sam.

"Oh, my goodness!" gasped his mother. "Where did you find that treasure?"

"I found the diamond on the rubbish heap," said the little cockerel. "But a large king stole it. The rest of the stuff I found in the king's treasure chest. I guess he stole that too."

"You are a clever little cockerel!" said Sam. "Very clever indeed!"

The next day Sam's mother took the treasure to town and sold it. And then she and Sam shared the money with all the poor people they knew.

Ever after, Sam and his mother and the little cockerel lived together happy and content. And, of course, the cockerel never again had to go and scritch-scratch on the rubbish heap to find his breakfast!

Little Red Hen and the Rascally Fox

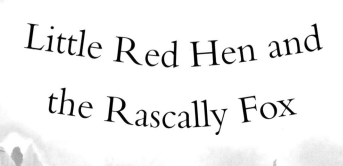

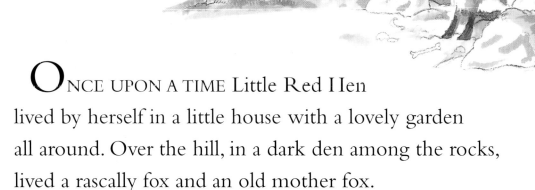

ONCE UPON A TIME Little Red Hen
lived by herself in a little house with a lovely garden
all around. Over the hill, in a dark den among the rocks,
lived a rascally fox and an old mother fox.

This rascally fox thought Little Red Hen would make a
very tasty dinner, so he kept trying to catch her. But Little
Red Hen was too clever for him. Every time she left
home, she locked the door behind her, *and* every time she
came back, she locked the door behind her *and* put the
key in her apron pocket where she kept her scissors,
needle and thread, and a piece of sugar candy.

At last, one night when he was lying in his den, the rascally fox worked out a way to catch Little Red Hen.

Early the next morning, he said to the old mother fox, "When I come home, have the pan on the fire, with the water boiling, because today, for sure, I shall bring back Little Red Hen!"

Then he slung a bag over his shoulder, and away he ran, until he came to Little Red Hen's garden. Then in he crept and hid behind some bushes.

After a while Little Red Hen opened the door. She looked about, but she couldn't see anyone. So she stepped over to the wood pile and quickly picked up some sticks for her fire.

As soon as her back was turned, the rascally fox slipped into the house…and hid behind the door.

A few moments later, Little Red Hen hurried back
in. She dropped the sticks, and closed the door. She was
just going to lock it when she heard – *swish-swish-swish!*
And then she saw the rascally fox, with the bag slung over
his shoulder, and his long bushy tail spread out behind
going *swish-swish-swish!*

She was scared! But – *whoo-oosh!* she flew straight up
to the wooden beam near the ceiling and perched there.

"Ah-ha! You may as well go home," she said. "You
can't and you won't catch me, you rascally fox!"

"Ah-ha! Can't I?" said the rascally fox.

And he began to whirl round and round in a circle,
after his own tail. Faster, faster, faster he whirled until poor
Little Red Hen got so dizzy with watching, that *plop!* she
dropped off the beam and landed on the floor.

Then the rascally fox picked her up, stuffed her in the bag, slung the bag over his shoulder, opened the door, and away he ran.

Poor Little Red Hen was all smothered and hot inside the bag. So she took her scissors out of her pocket and *snip! snip!* she cut a hole in the bag, stuck her head out and looked around.

Now, with all the running and whirling, the rascally fox began to feel tired, so he stopped for a rest. And the next thing, he began to snore. *Hunch-chrrr! hunch-chrr!*

Then…*snip! snip! snip!* Little Red Hen cut the hole bigger and jumped out. She found a big stone and pushed it into the bag. She took out her needle and thread, and quickly stitched up the hole. Then she ran home, as fast as she could.

When she got there, she locked the door behind her. "Ah-ha!" she chuckled. "You couldn't and you didn't catch me, you rascally fox!" And then she ate a piece of her favourite sugar candy.

Now, as soon as he woke, the rascally fox was off, carrying the bag, the same as before. He never guessed there was only a big stone in it.

When he came to his dark den among the rocks, he
said to the old mother fox, "Have you the pan on the fire?
And is the water boiling?"

"The water is bubbling and steaming," she said. "But
have you got Little Red Hen?"

"I have! She's in the bag," he said. "Now let's boil her
up for our dinner!"

The old mother fox took the lid off the pan. The rascally
fox lifted the bag, gave it a shake and out fell – A BIG
STONE!

Kersplash! Boiling water splashed and sploshed all over
the rascally fox and the old mother fox and scalded them
to death. So that was the end of them.

But Little Red Hen lived happily ever after, in her own
little house with the lovely garden all around.

Silkypaws and the Three Little Kittens

SILKYPAWS HAD THREE little kittens. Snowy was mostly white, Sooty was mostly black and Smoky-grey was mostly grey. They were beautiful kittens, but they were always up to mischief, always poking their little noses into anything new.

One day those three little kittens were full of mischief, climbing and jumping, wrestling and chasing. They made their mother, Silkypaws, feel so very tired that she sat down, closed her eyes and fell fast asleep.

Waving their tails in the air, the three little kittens tiptoed off into the kitchen, and…a white mouse scampered by.

Whippity-quick! the kittens chased her. The white mouse dived into a big flour bin, and the kittens dived in after her. WHOO-OOF! There was flour all over them. Such a mess! But they couldn't see the white mouse anywhere. She was safely back in her own mouse hole.

Three floury-white kittens scrambled out of the flour bin and ran to their mother. MIAOU!

Silkypaws opened one sleepy eye, and she said:

"Three white kittens! You're not my kittens –

Snowy, Sooty and Smoky-grey!"

Then she closed her eye and fell fast asleep.

Waving their tails in the air, the three little kittens were just going to tiptoe off again, when…a black bird flew in through the open window.

Whippity-quick! the kittens chased him. The black bird flew to the fireplace and up the chimney, and the kittens climbed up the chimney after him. WHOO-OOF! There was soot all over them. Such a mess! But they couldn't see the black bird anywhere. He had flown out of the chimney and was safely back in his own nest.

Three sooty-black kittens scrambled down the chimney and ran to their mother. MIAOU!

Silkypaws opened one sleepy eye, and she said:

"Three black kittens! You're not my kittens –
Snowy, Sooty and Smoky-grey!"

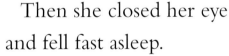

Then she closed her eye and fell fast asleep.

Waving their tails in the air, the three little kittens tiptoed through the kitchen and into the garden, and…a green frog hopped by.

Whippity-quick! the kittens chased her. The green frog hopped across the slippy-sticky mud and in among the rushes by the pond, and the kittens scampered after her. WHOO-OOF! There was mud all over them. Such a mess! But they couldn't see the green frog anywhere. She was safely swimming in her own pond.

Three muddy-grey kittens scampered back across the mud and ran to their mother. MIAOU!

Silkypaws opened one sleepy eye, and she said:

"Three grey kittens! You're not my kittens —
Snowy, Sooty and Smoky-grey!"

Then she closed her eye and fell fast asleep.

Waving their tails in the air, the three little kittens tiptoed through the kitchen and into the garden. No white mice ran by. No black birds flew by. No green frogs hopped by. But…it began to rain. The kittens didn't like this wet stuff that was falling on them.

They just scooted across the garden and back inside.
But…the rain washed off the grey mud…it washed off
the black soot…and it washed off the white flour…

Then three little kittens, one mostly white, one mostly
black and one mostly grey ran to their mother. MIAOU!

Silkypaws opened one sleepy eye, and she said:

"Poor wet kittens! My very own kittens –
Snowy, Sooty and Smoky-grey!"

Then she opened both eyes. "Come, my little kittens,"
she said. And very gently she licked her three beautiful
kittens, all over, until their fur was soft and dry.

Then the kittens curled up beside their mother and
cuddled close. Silkypaws purred: *"Prrrr…prrr…"* The
kittens purred: *"Prrrr…prrr…"* And before long those
three little kittens were as quiet and good as could be,
because…they were fast asleep.

AFTERWORD

All these Sleepytime Stories have their roots in favourite traditional tales. Down the years, storytellers around the world have told them to children in many different ways. In my turn, I have told them afresh, adapting and adding new twists and flourishes to entertain and delight today's children.

The Turtle Who Ran Away is based on a tale told by the Native American Hopi. *Speckledy Hen Bakes a Cake* is based mainly on a North American source. *Anna and the Shaggy Bear*, *Little Mouse Twitchy Whiskers* and *Silkypaws and the Three Little Kittens* have Russian tales as their starting point. *The Three Billy Goats Gruff* and *Tom's Naughty Little Donkey* have been retold from Norwegian stories, and *Robin Redbreast's Song* from a Scottish story. A West African setting has been given to *Twenty Cheeky Monkeys*, an English tale much changed. *Three Magic Wishes* is a story well known throughout most of Europe. *Leo Lion and Molly Mouse* comes from Aesop. *Big Grumps Frog* is based on an Australian Aboriginal story. *Little Peachling and the Giants* has long been a great favourite in Japan. *King Saggy-Baggy-Pants and the Sparkly Diamond* is Hungarian. An Irish/American poem by Horace E. Scudder is the main source for *Little Red Hen and the Rascally Fox*.